Who Is Sleeping In Aunty's Bed?

Story by
Kathy Stinson

Pictures by
Robin Baird Lewis

Toronto   Oxford   New York

Oxford University Press

1991

Oxford University Press, 70 Wynford Drive, Don Mills, Ontario, M3C 1J9

Toronto   Oxford   New York   Delhi   Bombay   Calcutta   Madras   Karachi
Petaling Jaya   Singapore   Hong Kong   Tokyo   Nairobi   Dar es Salaam
Cape Town   Melbourne   Auckland

and associated companies in
Berlin   Ibadan

Canadian Cataloguing in Publication Data

Stinson, Kathy
Who is sleeping in aunty's bed?

ISBN 0-19-540824-1 (bound)   ISBN 0-19-540852-7 (pbk.)

I. Lewis, Robin Baird.   II. Title.

PS8587.T56W5   1991   jC813'.54   C91-093083-X
PZ7.S75Wh   1991

For Ann, Cammie, Peter,
Nicholas, Adrian,
Taylor and Rosemary
–K.S.

For Kyla and Sarah
in memory of Ewart and Esme's cottage
at Shanty Bay
–R.B.L.

"Tonight it's my turn to sleep with Aunty," said Meg.

"No, it's my turn," argued Nicole.

Dad flipped a coin and Meg won.

Everything in Aunty's house was quiet until . . .

Aunty snorted and Meg woke up.

Aunty's open mouth fluttered noisily.
Meg rolled over. She covered her ears with her pillow.
But still, she could hear Aunty's snoring.
Meg was wide awake.

Meg held Aunty's lips together
to stop them from flapping.
But the noise from her nose
was worse.

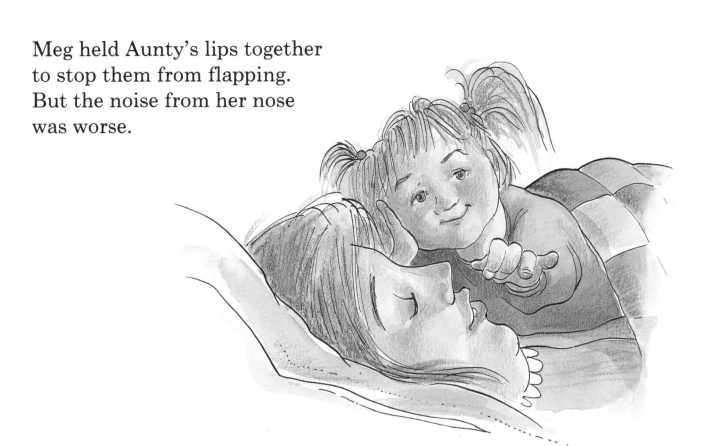

Meg stuck her head underneath two pillows.
Still, she could not sleep.

"I'm so tired," thought Meg. "I want to go to sleep,
but Aunty's snoring is shaking the bed.
There is only one thing for me to do."

Meg tumbled out of Aunty's bed. *Creak.*

She tiptoed past Nicole, asleep on the couch.

She tiptoed into the guest room.
She crawled into bed between her parents. *Mmmm.*
And went to sleep.

Everything in Aunty's house was quiet until . . .

Meg kicked Mom and Mom woke up.

Meg stretched out.
Mom moved over, closer to the wall.
Meg's elbow flopped up and hit Mom in the ear.
Mom was wide awake.

Mom pushed Meg's arms and legs
back to the middle of the bed.
But Meg flailed about even more.
Mom tried to make herself very small.
Still, she could not sleep.

"I'm so tired," thought Mom.
"I want to go to sleep,
but there are too many elbows
and too many knees in this bed.
There is only one thing for me to do."

Mom rolled out of bed and left the guest room.

She tiptoed past Nicole,
asleep on the couch,
into Aunty's room.

Gently she lifted the covers
and slipped into bed beside Aunty.
Cre-ee-eak. Mmmm.
And went to sleep.

Everything in Aunty's house was quiet until . . .

Mom sang out in her sleep, "My only sunshine,"
and Aunty woke up.

In her sleep Mom continued, "You make me happy . . ."

"Just like when we were kids," thought Aunty.
Aunty finished the song.
"Please don't take my sunshine away."

Finally Mom was quiet.
But Aunty was wide awake.

Aunty tried counting sheep. "One, two, three . . ."

But Mom rolled over and mumbled,
"Love you, honey."

Aunty kept counting her sheep.
"Three hundred and forty,
three hundred and forty-one . . ."
Still, she could not sleep.

"I'm so tired," thought Aunty. "I want to go to sleep.
I don't want to count and I don't want to sing.
There is only one thing for me to do."

Aunty crawled out of her bed. *Cre-eak*.

She tiptoed over to Nicole,
asleep on the couch.
She lifted Nicole off the couch
and put her in bed beside Mom.
Creak.

Then Aunty slipped into
the warm sleeping bag on the couch.
Mmmm.
And went to sleep.

Everything in Aunty's house was quiet until . . .

Nicole took all the blankets and Mom woke up.

Nicole tucked the blankets up tight under her chin.
Mom shivered and pulled on the corner of the blankets.
Nicole sighed and smiled in her sleep.
But Mom was wide awake.

Mom tried to unroll the blankets from around Nicole.
Nicole and the blankets fell onto the floor.
Mom got out of bed. *Cre-ee-eak.*
She lifted Nicole back into bed. *Creak.*
She climbed back into bed. *Cre-ee-eak.*
Still, she could not sleep.

"I'm so t-t-tired," thought Mom.
"I want to go to sleep.
But it's too c-c-cold in this b-b-bed.
There is only one thing for me to do."

Mom flopped out of Aunty's bed. *Cre-ee-eak*.
She tiptoed past Aunty, asleep on the couch,
to where Meg was sleeping with her dad.
She carried Meg to Aunty's bed
and laid her down beside Nicole,
who had kicked off the blankets. *Creak*.

She covered both the girls and kissed them goodnight.
Then Mom went back to the warm place beside Dad.
Mmmm.
And went to sleep.

Everything in Aunty's house was quiet until . . .

the sun came in and Nicole woke up.

Nicole stared at Meg until Meg woke up too.

"What am I doing in bed with you?" said Nicole.
"I went to sleep on the couch."

Meg shrugged. "I went to sleep with Aunty,
and then with Mommy and Daddy."

"We're in Aunty's bed now," said Nicole.

"But where is Aunty?" asked Meg.

"There is only one thing for us to do."

Meg and Nicole scrambled out of bed. *Creak. Creak.*
They crept into the living room.
There was Aunty, asleep on the couch.

Nicole pulled up Aunty's eyelids.
"Are you asleep?" she asked.

"Not any more," said Aunty.

Meg and Nicole giggled and snuggled
deep into Aunty's sleeping bag.
Aunty giggled too.

All the noise woke Mom. She got up
to join everyone, giggling on the couch.

Then Dad came. He rubbed his eyes.

"Did everyone have a good sleep?"

"Tonight it's my turn to sleep with Aunty," said Nicole.

Cre-ee-ee-eak. Creak.

Mmmm.